the hungry ghosts

Julius Lester

pictures by Geraldo Valério

Dial Books for Young Readers

DIAL BOOKS FOR YOUNG READERS
A division of Penguin Young Readers Group
Published by The Penguin Group
Penguin Group (USA) Inc., 375 Hudson Street, New York, NY 10014, U.S.A.

Penguin Group (Canada), 90 Eglinton Avenue East, Suite 700, Toronto, Ontario, Canada M4P 2Y3 (a division of Pearson Penguin Canada Inc.) • Penguin Books Ltd, 80 Strand, London WC2R 0RL, England • Penguin Ireland, 25 St. Stephen's Green, Dublin 2, Ireland (a division of Penguin Books Ltd) • Penguin Group (Australia), 250 Camberwell Road, Camberwell, Victoria 3124, Australia (a division of Pearson Australia Group Pty Ltd) • Penguin Books India Pvt Ltd, 11 Community Centre, Panchsheel Park, New Delhi - 110 017, India • Penguin Group (NZ), 67 Apollo Drive, Rosedale, North Shore 0632, New Zealand (a division of Pearson New Zealand Ltd) • Penguin Books (South Africa) (Pty) Ltd, 24 Sturdee Avenue, Rosebank, Johannesburg 2196, South Africa • Penguin Books Ltd, Registered Offices: 80 Strand, London WC2R 0RL, England

The publisher does not have any control over and does not assume any
responsibility for author or third-party websites or their content.

Designed by Nancy R. Leo-Kelly
Text set in Cochin
Manufactured in China on acid-free paper
1 3 5 7 9 10 8 6 4 2

Library of Congress Cataloging-in-Publication Data
Lester, Julius.
The hungry ghosts / Julius Lester ; pictures by Geraldo Valério.
p.   cm.
Summary: A resourceful young boy tries to help three hungry ghosts find something to eat.
ISBN 978-0-8037-2513-3
[1. Ghosts—Fiction. 2. Night—Fiction.] I. Valério, Geraldo, date, ill. II. Title.
PZ7.L5629Hu 2009   [E]—dc22   2008008695

The illustrations for this book were rendered in acrylic paint on watercolor paper.

To my sons, Malcolm and David,
and their children, Page, Teddy, Grant, and Yehuda Yair —J.L.

For Nicoli and Igor —G.V.

It was a night when the only creature out and about was Miss Big Eyes, who is also known as Sister Owl. It was a night when Sister Moon unfolded her arms to let her light pour down over the countryside like fresh milk on cereal. It was a night that was perfect for ghosts, and three ghosts in particular— Jessica, Byron, and Lamont.

They eased out of the ground, stopped, and looked around as if searching for something or somebody. Then they saw the house on the other side of the wall surrounding the cemetery. They smiled and drifted quietly through the moonlight, up to an open window, and into a room where Malcolm David lay sleeping.

He woke up shivering as a cold breeze came through the room. Something was wrong because it had been springtime when he went to bed. What was winter doing here when spring had just started making flowers bloom and grass green? But then the cold wind was gone.

"Goodness my gracious my gracious my goodness!" Malcolm David exclaimed. "What is going on?"

He got out of bed, looked out the window and across the big field next to his house. At the very end was a stone wall. On the other side of the wall was a cemetery where the tombstones gleamed dully like broken dreams.

"Those were ghosts who brought that cold wind in here," he said aloud. "What else could make spring feel like winter?"

Why had ghosts come in his room? he wondered. Had they been looking for something? And if so, what?

All the next day as he played in the field,
he kept glancing over the wall at the cemetery. He
couldn't see any ghosts, but he knew they were there.
Somewhere.

That evening Malcolm David got ready for bed before Sister
Moon had finished washing her face and Brother Sun was still
painting the western sky with colors nobody had names for. When
his parents saw him putting on his pajamas, they wanted to know
if he felt all right.

"I'm okay," he told them. "Just a little sleepy."

But, as soon as his parents closed his door, he got up and went
to the window. Sitting in a nearby tree was his ringring bird. This
is a very special bird. There used to be millions of them until the
alarm clock was invented. Now there are very few, but one of
them belonged to Malcolm David,
though his parents didn't know.
When his ringring bird saw him,
it flew to the windowsill.

"How can I help you?" the
bird asked the boy.

"I need you to wake me up so I can go see the ghosts."

The ringring bird looked at the sky. "Let me think," it mumbled. "Ghosts usually come out, if they're coming, about when Sister Moon is halfway between Not-Yet-Yesterday and Almost-Tomorrow. That's when I'll wake you up."

Malcolm David was sleeping soundly
when the ringring bird flew through the window
and landed on his head. "Hey! It's time to get up!"

"Thanks," he said. Malcolm David dressed quickly,
then went quietly out the back door.

He took a deep breath. Looking for ghosts had
sounded like a good idea, but now he wasn't sure. Before
he changed his mind, he climbed quickly over the wall.
Suddenly Sister Moon disappeared behind clouds that
had not been there a second before.

Brother and Sister Night hated the full moon because
it meant their children, Darkness and Fear, could not
go outside and play. But now, with clouds smothering
the moonlight, their children swooped down and began
covering houses and fields with a blackness as thick as
remorse for a hurt that can never be undone.

Malcolm David looked toward his house but couldn't
see it. Then, suddenly—

"OOOOOOO!"

Malcolm David started trembling. "Who said that?" he asked in a quavering voice.

"EEEEEEEE!"

He looked this way and that way, upway and downway, but didn't see anything.

"ARRRRRG!"

He started running, but with one foot wanting to go forward and the other wanting to go backward, and him just wanting to go, he tripped and fell.

"Oh, dear." It was the polite voice of Jessica.

"Is he all right?" asked Byron in his deep, male voice.

"No one has ever come looking for us," added Lamont.

Floating in the air directly over him, Malcolm David saw three very pale figures that looked like soft, thin clouds.

"Were you the—the ones making those scary noises?" he asked.

"What scary noises?" Byron wanted to know.

"OOOOOO! and EEEEEE! and ARRRRRG!" Malcolm David said, imitating the sounds.

"Is that why people run away when they hear us?" Jessica wondered. "We didn't know those sounds were scary."

"Then why do you make them?" Malcolm David asked, getting up and brushing the dirt from his pants.

"Well, we don't actually make the sounds," Jessica answered.

"Then who does?"

"It's our stomachs," Lamont said.

"Your stomachs?"

"Yes, our stomachs. We are hungry," Byron explained.

"Hungry!" the boy exclaimed.

"But you're ghosts. Ghosts don't have stomachs."

"And how would you know?" Jessica asked. "Are you a ghost?"

"Well, no."

"Don't *you* get hungry?" Lamont queried.

"Yes, but I'm alive!" the boy insisted.

"So?"

"What do you eat?" Malcolm David wanted to know.

There was a long silence. Then, all three ghosts started to sob.

"BOOHOOHOOHOO! We don't remember!" they cried together. "WE DON'T REMEMBERRRRRRRRR!"

And as suddenly as they had appeared, the ghosts disappeared, and the clouds began to move away from Sister Moon's face. Darkness and Fear ran back to their parents.

The next day all Malcolm David could think about was finding something for the ghosts to eat. But whatever he thought of you needed forks, spoons, knives, and teeth to eat. Ghosts didn't have teeth, and he didn't think they could hold utensils.

When his mother noticed him wandering around the house, she asked, "What are you doing?"

"Nothing."

"Well, what you ought to be doing is cleaning up that messy room of yours."

Clothes, books, and toys were scattered in piles across the floor of his room. Glasses with dried milk in the bottom were on his desk. A half-eaten bowl of cereal with blueberries in it was on his dresser. On the floor beside the bed were plates with orange rinds, banana peels, and apple cores on them. Malcolm David smiled. He sure knew how to make a mess!

By late afternoon the room was so clean, he figured he wouldn't have to clean it ever again.

That night when he got in bed, he was sad. He had so wanted
to find something to feed the hungry ghosts. But he had failed.

He had just snuggled beneath the covers when—

"Ouch!" "Get off me!" "That hurts!"

Malcolm David sat up. "Who said that?"

"We did!" came the emphatic response from tiny voices.

He flung the covers back and saw tiny balls of pale blue on the sheet.

"Who—who—who are you?"

"Blueberry ghosts."

"I beg your pardon?"

"You remember those blueberries in that yucky bowl of cereal that
was on your dresser? We're their ghosts."

The boy shook his head. "Whoever heard of blueberry ghosts?"

"That's the problem," another little voice responded. "Everybody
knows about people ghosts, but nobody cares about *us*. And we're
everywhere."

"You are?"

"Sure. You know when you're walking along and trip
for no reason?"

"I do that a lot."

"Well, you tripped over a ghost. It could have been
a grass ghost, a leaf ghost, or a flower ghost."

"I don't believe this," Malcolm David said.

The blueberry ghosts wafted up from the bed and began dancing around Malcolm David in a wide circle. Suddenly banana ghosts were dancing around his feet. Orange ghosts and apple ghosts were practicing gymnastics on his desk.

Suddenly Malcolm David smiled the most beautiful smile he had ever smiled. Quickly he got dressed. "Come on!"

The apple ghosts, orange ghosts, blueberry ghosts, and banana ghosts lined up in rows behind Malcolm David and off they went—down the stairs, across the yard, over the stone wall, and into the cemetery.

"OOOOOOOO!"
"EEEEEEEEEE!"
"ARRRRRRRG!"

The three ghosts appeared above Malcolm David's head.

"Hi!" he called out. "I think I know what you eat."

"Please tell us," Jessica begged him.

"Well, since you're ghosts, you have to eat ghost food, right?"

The three ghosts looked at one another.

"I think you may be right," Byron said.

"Well, look!" Malcolm David said, gesturing to
the apple, orange, blueberry, and banana ghosts
behind him.

"Oh, my!" Lamont exclaimed.

"They look positively delicious," Jessica said.

"They really, really do," added Byron.

The ghost fruit swelled with pride hearing themselves praised. The ghosts looked down at the ghost fruit and smiled. The ghost fruit looked up at the ghosts and smiled. As the ghosts floated down, the ghost fruit rose up. Ghosts and ghost fruit joined. The air began to glow brightly.

"What's going on?" Malcolm
David wanted to know, wondering if
it was time to be afraid.

"Don't be scared," Byron said. "Watch!
Now you'll see what ghosts *really* look like."
And he turned into a long shaft of blue
and white light that stretched from one
end of the cemetery to the other.

"Look at me," cried Jessica, and she turned into a disc of reddish orange light standing on end like a wheel, and it rolled around and around the cemetery.

"Look at us!" called Lamont and a chorus of tiny voices. A mass of sparkling lights rippled across the cemetery like a ribbon.

"Why, you're beautiful!" Malcolm David exclaimed.

"Thank you very much," the ghosts said, pleased. "Now watch!"

The shaft of light shrank and rolled itself into a ball. The disc flattened and rose into the air and began spinning around and around. The sparkling lights danced toward Malcolm David. He smiled as they came closer and closer until, softly, they covered him, and he sparkled like he was covered in diamonds.

With a great WHOOSH, the ghosts went upward and
wrapped themselves into a braid that shimmered against the night sky.
Then they were gone and there was only the night and the silence . . .

and a little boy, smiling.